# Affiliate Marketing Unlocked

Smart Way to Achieve Financial Freedom

Deepak Yadav

ISBN 978-93-5667-226-0
© Deepak Yadav 2022
Published in India 2022 by Pencil

*A brand of*

One Point Six Technologies Pvt. Ltd.
123, Building J2, Shram Seva Premises,
Wadala Truck Terminal, Wadala (E)
Mumbai 400037, Maharashtra, INDIA
**E** connect@thepencilapp.com
**W** www.thepencilapp.com



DISCLAIMER: *The opinions expressed in this book are those of the authors and do not purport to reflect the views of the Publisher.*

# Author biography

I am an infopreneur and i make money online.

I have seen many ups and downs in my life.

But the year 2016 was the worst time of my life because at this time I was very much troubled by depression and anxiety.

I made every effort to get out of this mental state.

Today I am far away from depression and anxiety.

In fact my life changed after the depression.

I learned many life lessons during this time and I want to teach this lesson to you through my books.

I hope you get to learn a lot from my books which might change your career and life.

# CONTENTS

# Introduction

Today's time is the time of online where all the work from buying to selling goods has started happening online today.

There are many platforms and brands around the world that sell their products through online medium.

There is no shortage of people buying online products in our country.

Millions of people also shop online through online reselling applications like Meesho and also sell their products.

But the question arises that which such marketing strategy is used by these platforms from which they get so much profit?

So the answer is affiliate marketing.

Affiliate marketing is being used by more than 80% of the brands today and they are also getting profit from it.

Affiliate marketing is the most powerful weapon to generate revenue, inside which many marketing tools are used and further in this book you will get to know about these mediums in detail.

If you have heard the name of affiliate marketing and do not know how it works or how to earn money from it, then this book is of great use to you.

You will also know the benefits of affiliate marketing, in which the biggest advantage is that despite having your own product, you will be able to earn money by selling the product or service of any other person, company and organization.

Although there are many strategies to do affiliate marketing, but in this book you will be told about the best affiliate marketing strategy.

If you have an active website or a good follower on social media, then you can make all your dreams come true by using it.

But if you do not use website and social media sites for affiliate marketing then you are missing out on a huge opportunity to earn money.

As we told you that affiliate marketing is used by online platforms around the world, then there are many options to earn money here.

You can get a good salary by selling the products and services of your favorite category and on the other hand if you become an affiliate marketing expert then no one can stop you from earning lakhs of rupees.

When it comes to affiliate marketing programs, many questions arise in the mind such as:

What is Affiliate Marketing?

How does Affiliate Marketing work?

What are the benefits of Affiliate Marketing?

What does it take to do affiliate marketing?

How can I earn money by becoming an expert in Affiliate Marketing?

So we are going to answer all the questions given here because these are such questions without knowing about which no affiliate marketing program can be successful.

The first important question in these questions is what is affiliate marketing?

Without understanding this, you will not understand any of the following information.

That's why first of all we will explain affiliate marketing in this guide of affiliate marketing.

But before starting this topic, know that affiliate marketing is not an easy task, but by understanding its strategy and doing it in the right way, you can easily earn money.

At the same time, the most important thing is that you have to read this book till the end so that you know everything about affiliate marketing from beginning to end.

So let us first understand what is affiliate marketing to know better how to earn money by doing affiliate marketing:

What is Affiliate Marketing?

Affiliate marketing is that important part of digital marketing which is doing important work for website and social media influencers.

Through this Influencers and Publishers are earning lakhs of rupees sitting at home.

Do you want to be one of these too?

So let's know what is Affiliate Marketing:

To understand Affiliate Marketing easily, you have to know its definition, which we are going to tell you now-

Affiliate marketing is an easy way to generate income through which a blogger, youtuber website owner and publisher joins the affiliate program of a company or organization to promote its product or service on its website or social media platform and increase its sales. And on every sale you get some commission from the company or organization.

Today, more than half of the brands in the world run affiliate marketing programs, that is, give people an opportunity to promote their products and help them increase their sales and earn money in return.

In simple words, if you tell, this is a way to promote a product online, in which you earn commission on selling the product.

As you know that today is the age of website in the world, so every brand, service and company has its own website in which they run affiliate program.

But here also there are many questions like how does affiliate marketing work? How to get money in it? etc., which we have answered in the next section.

If you have a website that is active or you have a lot of followers on social media platforms, then you can use them to do affiliate marketing and generate a lot of income.

This question must also be arising in the minds of many people that can you start affiliate marketing without a website?

So let us tell you that most of the people take the purchasing decision by checking the product reviews on the website, that is, they decide whether the product is worth buying or not.

That's why website plays an important role in the world of affiliate marketing, although affiliate marketing programs can be run on other social media platforms as well, but if you have an active website in which a lot of visitors come every month, then you are in more profit. .

There are many such affiliate programs that you can join absolutely for free, which we will talk about later.

Are you still in doubt about affiliate marketing program?

Now the question arising in your mind that what is an affiliate marketing program?

So let us tell you that affiliate marketing program is such a process run by a company in which it gives a unique link of the product to the publisher, blogger and website owner, which can be promoted by the influencer on its website or social media platform to make a sale. Have to help.

Simply put, the whole process of affiliate marketing is an affiliate program.

Now a big question comes that what is most important for affiliate program?

So let us tell you that three things are very important to do affiliate marketing and those three things are website, product and a high quality content which is related to your product.

Often people make this mistake that they choose the product for the website but ignore the high quality content for it, which becomes the biggest reason for the spread of affiliate marketing.

A good content has the power to bring more and more visitors to the website, so it should not be ignored at all.

Many people also do this that instead of choosing a single topic, they choose more than one topic, as a result of which they are not able to focus well on any one topic nor can they provide a good content to the visitors. Will be able

That's why you have to choose a topic on which you are interested and for which you have a lot of knowledge and most importantly it is related to your product, then only you will be able to earn money by running a good affiliate program.

So now you must have understood about affiliate marketing, what is it and if you want to know why affiliate marketing is beneficial and how to do it, stay tuned in this book.

Hopefully now you have got all the information about Affiliate Marketing and Affiliate Marketing Program and you will be curious to know more about it.

Now the question arises that how does affiliate marketing work and how to earn money here, so let us answer this question for you:

How does Affiliate Marketing work?

As we told you that in affiliate marketing, you have to promote the product by joining a company or organization.

So this company and organization provides you a unique link of your product or service which you have to add on your social media platforms or website.

Let us understand this as an example:

Suppose you have joined the affiliate program of Amazon Associate and you want to earn money by promoting its product.

So first of all you have to choose a product and add the link of that product on your website or social media platform.

If many people visit your website or social media site every day, then some of them will definitely be such who will click on this link and will reach the account of Amazon Associate from where they will be able to buy the product.

When a visitor will buy the product provided by you, then you will get some commission on the sale of each product.

This commission can be different in each affiliate program, the same commission received in affiliate marketing also depends on the category of the product, that is, if you are promoting a high quality product, then you get more commission on it. If you are promoting a local product, then you get less commission on it.

There are also many such programs which provide very high commission, we will also tell you about this further.

There are many companies like Amazon, Flipkart and Meesho which run affiliate programs, so which company to join here depends on you.

There will also be a doubt in the mind of many people whether it is right to do affiliate marketing?

So let us tell you that today is the time of online, that is to say that today online medium is used to buy and sell products, so if you use your active website for affiliate marketing. So he can become a better career option for you because from here you can earn up to lakhs of rupees by becoming an affiliate expert.

It also has many advantages, in which the biggest advantage is that if you do not have any product of your own and you want to do business, then you can generate commission by selling others' products.

Also, nowadays people have started spending more time on social media platforms, so doing affiliate marketing on social media platforms can also be very beneficial.

To do affiliate marketing, you also have to take care of some things like if you are doing affiliate marketing then you have to provide all the information about your product to the visitors.

Like what are the benefits of the product? What are the disadvantages of the product? What is the product category? What is its quality? e.t.c.

Only after seeing all these, a visitor decides to buy the product or not.

The stronger your product review, the more profit you will get and the best thing here is that you can earn more money by joining not only one affiliate program but many affiliate programs at once.

The better customer experience you provide to the people, the more benefit you will get here.

Through an optimize website, you can take out the entire cost of your house sitting at home, for which you do not even need to work hard.

Only once you have to put the link of your product on your website and all the further work is done by the organization because in affiliate marketing you only have to promote the product and all the workload of its delivery is with the organization or the company itself.

Also, there are doubts in the minds of people that how do they get the money they get in affiliate marketing?

So the thing to note is that different affiliate programs use different payment methods like under many affiliate programs you will get money through direct deposit and your money will be directly transferred to your bank account And there are many affiliate programs that pay out using online payment platforms like PhonePe.

At the same time, you also get the option of taking payment by check under many affiliate marketing programs.

Are you wondering whether there is a charge for joining the affiliate program or not?

So let us tell you that there are many such affiliate programs in which you can join the affiliate program absolutely free, but there are also many affiliate programs providing high commission in which you charge for registering, but other than this none Charge is not taken from you.

In this way we can say that affiliate marketing is a very good way to earn money without investment or with very low investment.

Here you have to keep one more thing in mind that many times it happens that the customer who buys the product wants to return it, then you do not get any commission for that product.

Suppose that if the commission for the sale of that product has arrived in your bank account, then it is deducted over time, so you have to use affiliate marketing strategy in such a way that there is no chance of returning the product.

How to earn money from Affiliate Marketing This question is also very big because before joining Affiliate Marketing, the first question that comes in the mind of any blog and publisher is how to earn money through Affiliate Marketing.

Especially it is very important to know for those bloggers who will do in this field and keeping this in mind, we have come up with 10 ways to do affiliate marketing which will help you to earn money if you want to know about these methods in detail. So you have to read this book till the end.

Now the question comes that how to do affiliate marketing because there are many ways to do affiliate marketing, out of which it is difficult to identify the best strategy.

That's why we have brought you here a list of better ways by which you will be all set to do affiliate marketing.

After knowing these top 10 methods, all the doubts you have about affiliate marketing will be cleared.

So let us know about these 10 ways one by one and tries to understand Affiliate Marketing

# 1. Create a Blog Using WordPress

You must have heard the name of WordPress before because it is the most famous site in the world of website, but there are very few people who know that affiliate marketing can also be done through WordPress and there are many affiliate programs for this. Is.

If you have a website on WordPress then you can easily start affiliate marketing here by promoting products, themes and plugins etc.

Here you will find wordpress. Com Affiliate Program, WordPress Premium Plugin Affiliate Program, WordPress Premium Theme Affiliate Program, WordPress Hosting Plan Provider Affiliate Program There are many programs that you have to promote by creating a blog in WordPress.

More than half of website owners or bloggers keep WordPress at the first position and make a good income by creating blocks in WordPress and joining WordPress Affiliate Program, where you can get up to 20% commission on every sale.

You can also join web hosting affiliate marketing program by creating a blog in WordPress because it is one of the most profitable topic in WordPress because a hosting is needed to build a website, so getting commission from here is even easier. goes.

So if you have a WordPress website or you are about to create it, then you can earn commission by promoting the hosting plan of any best hosting provider through your blog?

Under this, you get many high paying affiliate programs like Dreamhost Affiliate Program, Bluehost Affiliate Program, Hostgator Affiliate Program which provide you a good commission on every single sale of hosting.

On the other hand, if we talk about the theme affiliate program of WordPress, then it is also very beneficial for you.

As you know, a theme is a medium to attract visitors to the website.

Suppose your website is good but its theme is not good, even then visitors do not come to your website or come very less, so people also provide commission for promoting the theme through WordPress theme affiliate program, so if you do this If you join the affiliate program, then you can easily earn money by promoting them by creating a blog on WordPress.

You can also promote WordPress plugin through your blog, although the competition here is very high because new products keep coming in the world press marketplace every day, so you have to keep promoting the new plugin and for this you have to know that the market Which plug-ins are in high demand, so you have to stay updated.

If you are thinking of promoting a product by writing a block on WordPress, then you also have to take care of some things like affiliate programs in World Press provide their commission to people through PayPal account, so you have to create PayPal account. .

The best part here is that joining the affiliate program for WordPress is very easy and absolutely free.

Here you get a subscription to the newsletter from where you can access the latest coupon codes and useful promotional material, so you must subscribe to it.

In this way, by writing a blog on the WordPress website, you can create a lot of income by promoting different types of products.

These are some of the features that are necessary for every website, so the chances of its sale are very high, so you can easily start affiliate marketing by doing this work.

# 2. Create a YouTube Channel

As you know that YouTube is a very big social media platform where crores of people make videos every day or use this platform for entertainment.

At the same time, there are many people who use this platform to earn money, in which earning money from affiliate marketing is the most famous.

Many questions may be coming in your mind like how YouTube can be used for affiliate marketing or how does it work on YouTube etc.

So let's understand it in detail:

If you want to earn money through affiliate marketing, then you have to create your own channel on YouTube, through which channel you will promote high quality products and earn commission by generating their sales.

YouTube Affiliate Marketing is an online business in which you promote the recommended product or service through your created video by adding an affiliate link.

If we see what is the difference between affiliate marketing in website and YouTube, then let us tell you that the only difference between these two is that the platform for doing affiliate marketing changes, the rest of the work you have to do like link add in website. is done by doing.

Not only do they add affiliate links to their channel on YouTube, they also try to make people understand about it by making videos or tutorials related to that product, and most people go through these social media sites after the website to review any product. They like to visit the platform because from here they can easily understand how a product looks like, what is its quality and what are its other reviews.

Whenever a visitor comes to your YouTube channel and buys the product through that link, then you get commission, but for this also you will have to work a little hard.

If you already have a YouTube channel and it has a good number of subscribers, then your affiliate marketing business can run well.

But if you do not have a YouTube channel, then you have to create an affiliate channel and its process is exactly the same as to create a normal channel.

Just its goal is that here you have to upload a video of your recommended product or service and also add a link to that product or service in the caption.

You can upload and make videos on any category of products, but keep in mind that you should create a channel on any one niche, such as if you have knowledge related to technology, then you should start the work of affiliate marketing by choosing a product related to technology. It will be beneficial that such visitors will come to your channels who like to know about the gadgets of technology or they need any such product.

For this, you will also have to do a planning of making your video content because it is not necessary that you will start getting its results immediately, but if you go on doing your work according to a planning then you will get success quickly.

Here you have to decide on which topics you will prepare a video and what will be its fixed time etc.

After that you should join affiliate program.

When it comes to affiliate programs, you will find many affiliate programs on the internet that you can join and promote their products through videos on YouTube such as Amazon.

Amazon is very trustworthy and is an established company on which millions of people keep shopping online so if you start from here then you can get success quickly.

This is a very big ecommerce platform and here you will get the product of each category available, so you can start affiliate marketing by choosing any product as per your wish.

When you have selected your product, then you have to upload the video of that product from time to time and add affiliate link so that visitors buy your product through that link and you will get its commission.

In this way, affiliate marketing can also be started through YouTube.

# 3. Create an E-Book and Collect Email Address

E book means electronic book which we can read anytime and anywhere with the help of computer or mobile.

It can be read through any medium, online and offline and is available in many formats.

E-books have become very popular in today's time because there is no need to carry it anywhere like a book because it is downloaded in your smartphone itself.

There are many people who are earning money today by making eBooks but do you know that through affiliate marketing also money can be made using this medium?

If not, then let us explain how:

The first thing is that you have to create an e-book through MS Word and choose any product related to the topic of your book and promote it among your audience.

As you know that this is a book to be read online so here you can easily add affiliate link of any product and when your readers will buy the product through affiliate link then you will get commission.

Affiliate marketing through e-book is a very good way and very easy too.

Here you only have to choose a topic about which you have a good knowledge and after that you have to choose a product related to that topic or you can choose a product and create an e-book on it and add a link. By promoting the product.

You can also become a part of affiliate marketing by collecting email address through e-book or website.

You can put an email address collection page on your e-book which will be shown to the buyer of your e-book when he is reading your e-book.

This page will ask your readers for their email address and your readers will be able to read your e-book after registering their email address.

Similarly, by using the email registration box on the website, you can create a good email list which you will use for affiliate marketing.

You will be able to mail the audience about the new attractive product or offer of your e-book or any affiliate marketing program, as well as promote it by adding the affiliate link to the email.

When your readers or visitors click this link via email, they will be taken to the product's site from where they will be able to purchase the product.

The more people who buy your product, the more profit you will get.

Although you will get many email addresses from school, college or even from malls at very cheap prices, because often in such places a list of email addresses is prepared and sold and there are many web services that provide you email addresses in bulk. Such as godaddy, hosting, hostgator etc.

You can also create an email list using these services.

Today email marketing has become a huge part of affiliate marketing because most of the affiliate marketing reach their target audience through email marketing only.

It is not necessary that you collect email address only through website or e-book. You can also collect email address using social media platform.

You can upload an attractive offer or product post on social media and ask for an email address in the caption below.

Once your email list is ready, then you can easily reach your audience about attractive offers or product information through mail, we have explained this in further detail to you, so read this book till the end.

In this way e-book, website and social media site proves to be very beneficial to collect email address and also very easy way to do affiliate marketing where you can easily start affiliate marketing without any hard work.

What do I need to do for Affiliate Marketing?

Its list is not over here yet, you will get many tips through which you will be able to learn about affiliate marketing, so let's go ahead and know what you will have to do next to do affiliate marketing

# 4. List the product or service you love to buy

The most important thing in any business model is to choose the product or service because without it you will not be able to grow your business.

Similarly, it is very important to choose a product or service in affiliate marketing because unless you choose a right product, you will not be able to promote it properly nor will you get commission.

You can add to your list anything you use in your daily life that is easy to use and gives you a good experience.

To do affiliate marketing, first you have to prepare a list of those products or services that you yourself like to buy because you know better about it like how is that product profitable?

That's why you will be able to explain to people about that product very well.

There are many marketers who choose any random product, which they themselves do not know about, due to which they are not able to make the video of that product available to the people in the right way and some such important thing remains. Which is not able to present this product in front of the people properly.

The right way to do affiliate marketing is to choose a product or service about which you have knowledge of every aspect.

When you promote your favorite product yourself, then you can present all its features well in front of the people because you get the experience of how that product is helpful for you, as well as the knowledge of its quality. Which you can put in front of people in a very good way.

Here you can include any category of products in your list whether it is related to kitchen or technology or any other category because you will easily find affiliate programs on the internet for each category.

Before promoting any product, you should try using it yourself because until you do not have complete knowledge of that product, you will not be successful in affiliate marketing.

Therefore, first you should prepare a list of the product or service that you buy and use yourself.

It has many more benefits like you can earn money by joining affiliate program related to your favorite product which we will talk about in next section.

So the first thing you will do here is that you have to prepare a list of your favorite product or service that you want to promote so that you can get maximum profit.

Here you do not have to worry about the category because as we have already told you that today the demand for all types of products is increasing and the affiliate programs associated with it are also progressing rapidly.

# 5. Try to find out the best affiliate marketing network related to that product or service.

As you learned in the above section that first of all you have to make a list of the product of your favorite category, which you want to buy yourself, after which you have to try to know about the best affiliate marketing network related to this category of product or service. Have to do

Although you will find affiliate programs of every category on the Internet, but there are many such programs that provide you high commission, by joining which you can earn money easily.

The good thing is that you can join not only one affiliate program but more than one affiliate program and earn more money.

In affiliate marketing, you do not have any such restrictions where you join an affiliate marketing program, nor does this program force you to market your product only.

You can join more than one affiliate program by promoting more than one category of products whose knowledge you are well versed in.

In this way, you can join any one or more affiliate programs related to your product, let's understand it in detail:

Suppose you have prepared a list of a product in the fashion category that you want to buy yourself, then you will search on Google or any other medium about any affiliate network related to it.

As you know Amazon, Flipkart and Meesho are all online shopping apps where products of fashion category are easily available and their quality is also good, then you can join the affiliate program of any of these platforms. .

It may also happen that if you shop on Amazon or Flipkart yourself, then it will be even easier for you because you will already have the knowledge of the quality and price of the products available in these platforms.

So when you join the affiliate program of these platforms, then you can choose the product of your favorite fashion category from here and convert its affiliate link into short link and promote it by adding it to your website or social media platform. .

These are affiliate networks that provide you commission on every sale, so the commission you get is directly deposited in your bank account or given to you through online payment medium.

Now it comes to knowing which are the best affiliate networks in India from which you can earn more money by joining affiliate marketing programs, then read our next section carefully to know-

# 6. Top 5 Affiliate Networks

Although you will find many affiliate networks in India, whose affiliate program you can join, but here we will talk about the top five affiliate networks that you can earn high commission by joining, so let's go one by one to these top five affiliate networks. Know about-

Amazon Associate:

Amazon Associate, which is run by the world's largest ecommerce platform Amazon, is such an affiliate network in which you will get products of every category that you can promote.

Very few people know that Amazon is a great way not only to buy a product but also to earn commission by selling it and it is considered as one of the best affiliate marketing company.

You will find many reasons to use Amazon such as-

All types of products are available here.

You will not need to make much effort to sell Amazon product because it is a very popular company which is liked by people all over the world, so there is a possibility of selling your product by its name.

You will be getting the latest products all the time according to the trend, which you can promote and generate a lot of commission.

Its service is very good, so most people like to shop on Amazon.

Here the commission you earn depends on the sale of your product, that is, the more sales you increase, the more commission you will get, although its high commission rate is 10% per sale.

ClickBank:

If you work in the online field, then you must have heard the name of your click bank before.

At present it has more than 5 lakh members and ClickBank is more famous for its digital products.

If you join this network, then you can earn a good commission by promoting digital products.

It also has many benefits such as-

Here you will find digital products on which a lot of commission is provided.

It is also one of the best affiliate marketing company and its name has become popular all over the world.

Its commission rate is also very good which depends on the number of products done by you.

You will be surprised to know that ClickBank offers up to 75% commission.

eBay Affiliate Program:

When it comes to the eBay affiliate marketing program, it can also be trusted because eBay is a popular ecommerce company that sells both digital and physical products.

However, if you want to become a partner of the eBay Affiliate Program, then for this you have to create your account on EPN.

By becoming a partner here, you can promote any of its thousands of products that are related to your topic.

This affiliate program provides you commission from 1% to 5%, whose cookie duration is 24 hours i.e. if the visitor to your website has to buy that product within 24 hours, then only you get commission.

As its sales increase, you will get profit.

vCommission Affiliate Program:

VKMission is India's affiliate network in which more than one lakh affiliates have joined and under this program you will be able to create affiliate commission by selling the products of big e-commerce brands like Myntra, Snapdeal,

Airexpress.

When you join Affiliate Program of VCommission, here you get a minimum payment of Rs 1 thousand which is directly transferred to your bank account and this payment comes to your bank account after 2 months of the current month.

The point to note here is that if your commission is less than Rs 1 thousand, then it is given to you by rolling over it in the next month.

In this way, you can also get a good amount of money by joining the affiliate program of VCommission.

Bluehost Affiliate Program:

You must have heard about Bluehost because Bluehost is a hosting website that sells affordable hosting.

If you have bought hosting from Bluehost then you can understand how profitable it is and if till now you did not know that Bluehost also has an affiliate program then till now you were not aware of the huge opportunity.

The Bluehost affiliate program pays a commission of $65 on every sign up.

Bluehost also provides domain and free SSL certificate with its WordPress hosting which are very important for the website.

Here you will easily find ads and banners to advertise hosting, through which you will be able to easily promote the product on your site.

Its cookie duration is 3 months, which increases your chances of getting commission even more.

So these were the top five affiliate programs that you can easily get high commission by joining.

As you have learned in these five affiliate networks that these programs depend on the sale of the product, that is, the more you increase their sales, the more profit you will get, you can choose to join any program according to their cookie duration.

# 7. Promote Your Product or Service on Blog

If you work in the online field then you do not need to explain what is a blog and what role does it play in the world of website.

When it comes to affiliate marketing, promoting a product through a blog is the easiest and most beneficial.

So here you have to understand how a blog is created to promote any product or service and what are the things needed for this.

To create a good blog, you first need the topic of the blog on which you want to create an affiliate blog.

When you have chosen a good subject, then more than half of your trouble ends here.

An affiliate blog is one in which you promote the product of a company or organization by sharing new information on your website and earn commission and it is considered the best way to earn money.

To create a good blog, you also need to do keyword research which helps to rank your website on Google page, because till your site will not rank, then visitors will not come to it and neither will you visit your blog. You can earn commission by promoting a product.

You can attract more and more people to your affiliate blog by designing a good theme, hosting, and when you have prepared a good blog, then all you have to do is promote the product or service of the related company.

The most important thing here is how to write a good block because unless the quality of your blog is not good then you will not be able to run the affiliate program because it will not attract your visitors.

You need to do a lot of research to create a good block because when you read the content of big blogger then you come to know what things you need to add in your block and when you want to create a unique Once you have created a blog, you are all set to run an affiliate program.

When any person wants to buy a product, he first checks the review of that product and most of this work is done with the help of website, so if you promote these products through your blog then you will get many There are chances of getting visitors and some of these visitors are definitely those who buy the product through your affiliate link from which you get commission.

Along with this, by customizing any block, you can provide a better experience to the visitor.

There are many affiliate programs where you get a commission on every purchase of a visitor, that is, as many times as a visitor buys a product through your link, you are given a commission, so if you want a visitor to have a good experience with the help of your blog. If you are providing from this, then it is possible that that visitor will come to your own site again and again and use that link and buy the product, which will increase your profit even more.

So now you must have understood that how affiliate marketing can be done and money can be earned by promoting the product or service on the blog.

A blog plays a very important role in affiliate marketing because this is where you get most of the customers.

# 8. Promote your product or service on Youtube.

You have already learned a little bit about YouTube in the channel making section on YouTube, let us now understand it in more detail:

There are many online platforms like Flipkart, Amazon which provide you high commission to promote their product, so when you join the affiliate program of these programs then you can promote it on your youtube channel.

Suppose you have a lot of subscribers on your YouTube channel and every day your uploaded videos get good views, then you can easily promote your product or service here.

Let's understand this in the form of an example:

Suppose you have joined the affiliate program of Amazon Associate and you want to promote one of the products like mobile from here and want to earn commission, then you will first order this product for yourself and prepare its tutorial. Will upload on youtube.

You can easily tell everything about this mobile like which model is it? What are its merits? How is the quality of its camera? There are many more things that you can mention here.

Also you can add affiliate link of this mobile in the caption where your visitors will be able to order mobile by clicking on this link, the more people buy your product, the more profit you will get.

You easily get a lot of visitors on YouTube because it is a huge entertainment platform, as well as videos of related topics from each category are also available here, so if you choose a good topic and promote the product related to it on YouTube. If you do then you can easily earn money by doing affiliate marketing.

But here the question also comes that why would any visitor want to buy that product through your link?

Because the app from which you have ordered that product, visitors can also easily order the product through that app and the price is exactly the same, so how can you get commission?

So the answer is that when you add an affiliate link of a product to your social media platform and a visitor clicks on it and reaches that site, then you are providing a customer to the company for which you have been paid a commission. And a visitor will click on your affiliate link because he will easily click on that affiliate link and go directly to the side where he can buy the product so that he does not need to put much effort.

# 9. Promote your product or service through email marketing

Many times it happens that you try to do affiliate marketing through your website or social media platform but you are not able to get customers, then your affiliate program is not successful and many people also get disappointed.

So in such a situation, the question arises that what should we do so that we can promote our product or service and attract more and more customers?

So the answer is email marketing.

Email marketing is a huge part of digital marketing and plays an important role in affiliate marketing.

But the question arises that what is email marketing and how can affiliate marketing be done from here?

So let us tell you that email marketing is a way to promote a product or service through e-mail, for which you need at least 5000 email addresses.

Now you must be thinking that how to collect email address, then we have already told you in this book.

When you collect the email address, then you have to join any affiliate program and convey all the information about its product to your audience through mail.

Where you provide product information and its affiliate link on shot notice so that customers can buy your product through that link.

There is no such person who uses the internet and knows about email because more than 90% of the people use email at least once every month, so affiliate marketing can be done easily by collecting customers from here. can.

You promote your product or service directly to your customers, which increases the chances of success even more.

Here you can easily inform the audience about the attractive offers, coupon codes or discounts etc. of the affiliate program.

Also, it can also be run on automatic mode where from time to time your audience will be sending mail related to the product.

There are many tools through which email marketing can be done and automatic emails can also be sent such as convertkit, mailchimp, mailerlite etc.

In this way, affiliate marketing can also be done through email marketing.

# 10. Avoid This Mistake While Doing Affiliate Marketing

While doing affiliate marketing, there are many such mistakes which are very important to avoid because often people fail in affiliate marketing by making these mistakes.

Now we are going to tell you about these mistakes because these mistakes are very common, so let's try to know about them one by one:

First of all the mistake of the marketer is that they join too many affiliate programs at once because they want to earn a lot of money together but forget that by joining so many affiliate programs at once, they get each one. Affiliate program product has to be promoted which is a big challenge.

When you join any affiliate program, it is your responsibility that you will help to increase its sales, so if you join many affiliate programs, then every affiliate program's product is on you. The responsibility of selling comes due to which you can also come under stress.

The second biggest mistake is that affiliate marketers are unable to choose a right product and choose to promote any random product or service about which they themselves do not have much knowledge.

Many times it also happens that you start promoting a wrong product, then it is important that you choose a right product and promote it because if you provide the wrong product to the people, then gradually your website visitors will start decreasing. Because their trust will be removed from you, so you have to choose a product that you have used yourself or which you know well.

Another biggest and common mistake is that whenever someone joins affiliate program, he does not pay attention to his website only under the guise of earning money, that is, he does not pay attention to the content of his website.

Unless you put a high quality content on your website, your website neither ranks on the Google page nor visitors come to your site, so it is important that you put a high quality content on your website. And optimize it so that more and more people can visit your website and make your affiliate program successful.

Many people do this by copying and pasting the content on other blogs or website owner's site to put high quality content in their website and this is the biggest reason for the failure of affiliate marketing.

That's why you have to try that you write a high quality content yourself and put it in your website, only then you will be able to become a successful affiliate marketer.

The biggest reason for the failure of affiliate marketing is not paying attention to the performance of the website. You have to keep in mind that the visitors who visit your site visit your website only when your site is loaded at the right time.

If your site consumes too much time to load, then visitors do not wait on your website and go back, so it is important that you pay attention to the performance of your website and provide a good experience to the visitors so that the visitor has Have a reason to come back to your site.

# Conclusion

Affiliate marketing is a global industry which has proved to be the best business model for every brand.

Its reach is so much that if you want, even sitting in a small city of India, you can promote your product to America.

Only by generating traffic to the website, you step on the ladder of success because the more people who come to your site, the higher will be the chances of the affiliate program being successful.

The most important thing in any marketing is to reach the right audience and you have learned in this book how the target audience can be reached.

The best thing here is that you get a chance to earn commission by selling someone else's product without investment.

In any affiliate marketing, you are not asked about experience and qualification, so even if you are new in this field, you will not face any kind of problem, but for this it is necessary to have all the knowledge of affiliate marketing so that you can become a successful marketer.

When you look at the statistics related to affiliate marketing, you will come to know that how many affiliate marketers choose this career option but they fail very quickly due to lack of knowledge of the right strategy.

That is why it is very important that each of its strategies be seen and learned.

Here you have learned how affiliate marketing is done by avoiding small mistakes and this is also important because there are many reasons that directly affect affiliate marketing.

It is very important to understand these reasons and take necessary steps because unless you do not provide a good experience to the visitors of your site while doing affiliate marketing, neither they will click on your affiliate link nor will they buy the goods. The company will benefit and neither will you get commission.

In this way, every single aspect plays an important role in affiliate marketing, without knowing about which money cannot be earned by doing affiliate marketing.

Knowing what to do and what not to do in affiliate marketing is also important because even a small mistake of yours can spoil your entire affiliate program.

So now if you want to earn money from affiliate marketing, then make sure to take care of everything mentioned here.

Hope you liked the book Affiliate Marketing: Make Money Online and Achieve Financial Freedom and inspire you to move forward.

Along with this, we also hope that you have got the answers to all the questions related to affiliate marketing and there is no doubt in your mind.

If you want to know about new strategies to earn money in this way, then stay connected with us as we will continue to present new ways to earn money online.